CLASS CONFUSION

by Sarah Willson
illustrated by Robert Dress

SIMON SPOTLIGHT/NICKELODEON
New York   London   Toronto   Sydney

Stephen Hillenburg

Based on the TV series *SpongeBob SquarePants*® created by Stephen Hillenburg as seen on Nickelodeon®

SIMON SPOTLIGHT

An imprint of Simon & Schuster Children's Publishing Division

1230 Avenue of the Americas, New York, New York 10020

Manufactured in the United States of America

10 9 8 7 6 5 4 3

ISBN-13: 978-1-4169-1239-2

ISBN-10: 1-4169-1239-8

"SpongeBob, look out!" shrieked Mrs. Puff. But it was too late.
SCREEEECH! CRASH! BOOM! BOOM! BOOM!

"Oops. Sorry, Mrs. Puff," said SpongeBob. "I guess I forgot to put my blinker on. Looks like I failed my boating test . . . again."

"I'm calling in sick tomorrow," Mrs. Puff muttered. "I need a little 'me' time."

The next day SpongeBob arrived early for boating school, as usual. He breathed in deeply as he entered the front doors. "Behold the halls of learning," he said to himself.

"And here is the fountain of learning, which I drink from every day!" He took a sip from the drinking fountain, then continued down the hall.

At the classroom door SpongeBob's voice quavered. "And inside that room is the one who makes it all happen."

Slowly he pushed open the door. "Yes, indeed, inside this room is my teacher, the one and only Mrs. . . . AHHHHHHHH!"

Mrs. Puff was not at her desk! Instead there was . . . a *substitute!*

"Wh-wh-where's Mrs. Puff?" SpongeBob finally asked.

The substitute did not even look up from the magazine he was reading.

"Out today," he said, turning a page. "Have a seat."

SpongeBob sank heavily into his chair.

"Psssst!" said a voice next to him. It was Horace.

"I have a really funny idea," whispered Horace. "Let's play a trick on the sub! I'll pretend to be you, and you pretend to be me! Okay? It'll be hilarious!" Horace said, snickering.

"Uh, I guess so," said SpongeBob. He really didn't mind.

The substitute stood up. He was holding a clipboard. "Time to take attendance," he said. "Susie?"

"Here!" said Susie.

"Franco?"

"Here!" said Franco.

"SpongeBob?"

"HERE!" yelled Horace, before SpongeBob could say anything.

"Horace?" There was a pause. "Is Horace here today?"

SpongeBob felt a poke in his ribs. "Oh, yeah. Here," said SpongeBob, as Horace snickered some more.

The substitute began passing out pieces of paper. "Today you're supposed to take a test," he said.

Everyone groaned, except SpongeBob, whose eyes shone with excitement. A test!

"Don't forget to write your names at the top," said the substitute, before sitting back down at his desk.

"Pssst!" whispered Horace to SpongeBob. Horace pointed to his own test where he had written the name *SpongeBob*. Then Horace pointed at SpongeBob's paper.

SpongeBob wrote *Horace* at the top of his own test.

After the test, the substitute told the class, "Okay, now, open your manuals and read or something."

SpongeBob's hand shot up. "Mrs. Puff usually reviews the homework with us, and then after that she teaches us the lesson of the day and whoever has the most class participation—usually me—gets to stay after school and clap the erasers."

The substitute blinked at SpongeBob. "Is that right"—he looked down at his clipboard—"Horace? Well, *I* do things a bit differently. But you just reminded me. Your teacher left me a list of students who are to stay after school for extra help." He glanced at a sheet of paper. "Oh. Just one student. That would be you, SpongeBob." He pointed at Horace.

Horace looked over at SpongeBob and winked.

After school SpongeBob walked home very slowly.
"Hey, SpongeBob!" called Patrick. "Why the sad face?"

"Mrs. Puff wasn't at school today," SpongeBob began, "and there was a sub who didn't do anything the right way, and I was supposed to stay after school for extra help, but Horace was pretending to be me so he got to stay and I–," SpongeBob burst into tears.

Patrick patted his friend on the back. "Don't worry, SpongeBob," he said. "I'm sure Mrs. Puff will be back tomorrow and everything will be back to normal. You'll be failing another driving test before you know it!"

"I hope so," SpongeBob said, sniffling.

The next day SpongeBob held his breath as he entered the classroom. There, sitting at her desk, was his beloved Mrs. Puff! She was looking well-rested.

"Oh, Mrs. Puff!" gushed SpongeBob. "I sure am glad to see you!"

Mrs. Puff smiled. "Yes, I feel very refreshed after my, um . . . *sick day*," she said.

"Mrs. Puff, the sub forgot to give us homework, even though I reminded him three times!" said SpongeBob.

But Mrs. Puff wasn't listening. She was staring at a note. "Hmm . . . it seems that the substitute gave you all the *final exam* by mistake. And instead of keeping one student after school for extra help, he sent that student to retake his driving test."

All the color suddenly drained from her face. "And that student *passed* his driving test!"

"Who was the student?" Franco asked.

Mrs. Puff paused before announcing, "It was . . . *SpongeBob!*"

Everyone gasped. SpongeBob had passed his driving test at last!

"I passed! I passed! I passed at last!" SpongeBob yelled to everyone as he walked home—even though he didn't remember taking the test again.

"Hey, no more school, SpongeBob!" said Patrick. "We can play all day!"

SpongeBob grinned. "Yeah, that's great, Patrick! No more homework, no more school, no more . . . Mrs. Puff?" Suddenly he realized what this meant.

"Oh, no!" he wailed.

The next day SpongeBob forgot about Mrs. Puff for a while. He was too excited to get behind the wheel of a boat all by himself! "I'm ready! I'm ready!" he shouted.

A small crowd had gathered to watch SpongeBob drive alone for the first time. He had rented a limited edition Halibut GXT for this special occasion. Even Mrs. Puff was there. "I just don't understand it," said Mrs. Puff to herself. "How did he manage to pass his driving test? It's time for me to move far away. I don't want to be around when SpongeBob is driving!"

Vroom-vroom! SpongeBob revved up the engine. Then he noticed his teacher standing nearby. His heart grew heavy. He started to tear up.

"Even though I'm really glad I finally got my license, I sure am going to miss being in your class, Mrs. Puff," he said. "Good-bye, Mrs. Puff!"

SpongeBob stepped on the gas pedal and the boat flew forward and screeched to a halt in the middle of the intersection.

Suddenly a siren wailed and a police cruiser zoomed up. Two officers hopped out.

"Hey, you didn't stop at that stop sign," said one officer. "License, please."

"Yes sir, officer!" SpongeBob replied. "Here it is, brand-new and never used!"

The officer studied the license. "Hmm . . . seems there's a problem," he said. "You passed the *driving* portion of the boating test, but you failed the written exam."

SpongeBob looked at the test that the officer was holding up. Of course! It was the test that *Horace* had taken, pretending to be SpongeBob, and Horace had failed! And Horace must have passed the driving test . . . *while pretending to be SpongeBob!*

"I'm afraid you'll have to go back to boating school," the officer said.

SpongeBob started to sob. Even Mrs. Puff felt bad.

"Aw, don't cry, SpongeBob," said Mrs. Puff. "You'll get your license one day."

"No, Mrs. Puff," said SpongeBob. "I'm crying because I'm so happy! I thought I'd never see you again!" And he leaped out of the boat and into the arms of his startled teacher.

"I need a vacation," moaned Mrs. Puff softly.